For Tom, Joanna, Peter, Jack,
and the real Mr. K and Yudi

Library of Congress Cataloging-in-Publication Data
Stanton, Karen.
Mr. K and Yudi / by Karen Stanton.
p. cm.
Summary: When his master gets sick and then disappears
from their apartment, Yudi the dog searches faithfully for him.
ISBN 0-307-10210-6 (alk. paper)
1. Dogs—Juvenile fiction. [1. Dogs—Fiction. 2. Pets—Fiction.
3. Nursing homes—Fiction.] I. Title.
PZ10.3.S7808 Mr 2001   [E]—dc21   00-056168

*The illustrations for this book were created with acrylic paint
and collage on paper.*

Mr. K and Yudi

by Karen Stanton

A Golden Book • New York
Golden Books Publishing Company, Inc.
New York, New York 10106

Mr. K and Yudi were family . . . and the best of friends. They went everywhere together.

Each morning Mr. K laced up his walking shoes. Then he and Yudi shuffled out the door of their house, past Mrs. Dorothea's garden where Yudi liked to bury his best bones, down to Maxine's Bakery for peppermint tea and bear claws.

In the afternoons they listened to opera at home.

Later, Mr. K and Yudi sat together under the big walnut tree in the park to watch the sun set.

For dinner, Mr. K and Yudi ate at Penny's Diner. Yudi always sat under the table by Mr. K's left leg where he could see Penny serving the customers in her red high-tops. Yudi always had meatballs—extra large, no sauce.

Back home after dinner, Yudi brought Mr. K his blue slippers with the chew marks on the left toe. They sat by the fire together—Mr. K in his comfortable chair and Yudi on his favorite rug, sipping warm milk and dreaming.

Mr. K remembered the good old days when Mrs. K was still alive. Yudi dreamed up new ways to scare the squirrels in the walnut tree.

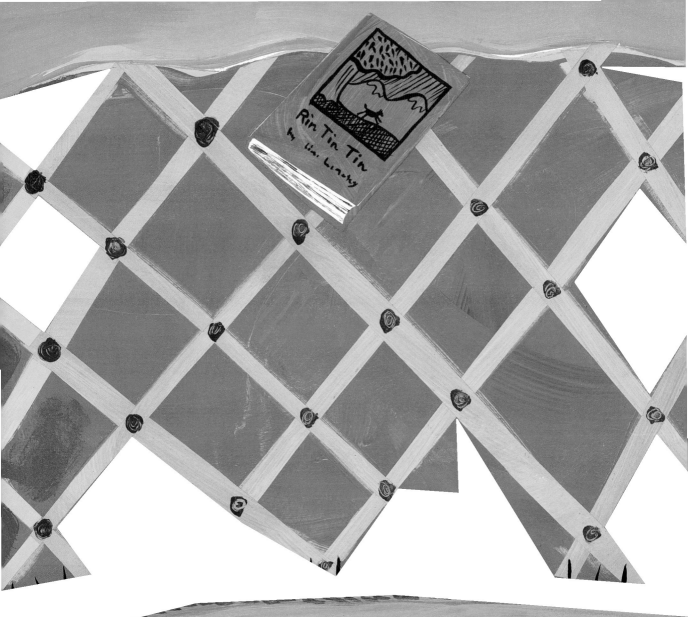

At 10:00, Mr. K got up from his comfortable chair, took his medicine, and shuffled into the bedroom for the night. Yudi always circled around three times to find the best spot on his pillow next to Mr. K's bed. After the second bedtime story, Mr. K reached down to scratch Yudi behind the ears and said, "You're a good one, Yudi." And Yudi always licked Mr. K on the hand. That was good night.

One day Mr. K did not get out of bed. Yudi stayed by his side all morning, but Mr. K did not get up. Yudi was listening to Mr. K's soft snoring and dreaming of bear claws and extra-large meatballs, when he realized he was in great need of a fire hydrant. He licked Mr. K's hand and headed off for the park, where he kept an eye out for the dogcatcher's shiny black boots.

Yudi was so busy chasing the squirrels in the walnut tree, he lost track of time.

It was dusk when Yudi hurried back home and heard a frightening sound—complete silence. No snoring, no opera music, no crackle of a fire in the fireplace, not even a shuffle of slippers. Yudi raced to Mr. K's bedroom and jumped up on the bed. The sheets and blankets were rumpled and the pillow was still warm, but Mr. K was gone.

Yudi frantically searched the house. Mr. K's tweed jacket and felt hat were still hanging by the front door, and next to them rested his cane. The only things missing were Mr. K and his blue slippers.

Yudi waited for Mr. K to return. After two long days with no meatballs, no music, and no scratches behind the ears, Yudi heard a key in the lock. The door swung open, but instead of shuffling footsteps, Yudi heard the clack-clack of high heels. He hid under Mr. K's bed. The high heels clacked around the house followed by a pair of clomping work boots.

"Pack it all up, Henry," said the high-heel person. The man in work boots began filling boxes with Mr. K's opera records, his books and pictures, even Yudi's favorite fireside rug. Yudi knew then that Mr. K was not coming back. Nobody even noticed as he slipped away in search of a man wearing blue slippers.

Yudi trotted by Mrs. Dorothea's garden, where he saw a gentleman in a felt hat and a tweed jacket chatting over the fence with Mrs. D.

On his feet the man wore wingtips. On his face he wore a crooked grin. Definitely not Mr. K.

Yudi passed Maxine's Bakery and heard a voice ordering peppermint tea and a bear claw. On his feet the man wore sandals. On his face he wore a long red beard. Definitely not Mr. K.

Yudi looked through the window of Penny's Diner and saw a man sitting at Mr. K's regular table. On his feet he wore cowboy boots. On his arm he wore a tattoo. Definitely not Mr. K.

There was only one place left to look. Yudi approached the park at sunset and saw a man standing near the walnut tree. On his feet he wore shiny black boots. On his sleeve he wore a badge. Definitely not Mr. K.

Yudi recognized those boots. He ran and the shiny black boots followed him. He ran away from the walnut tree, past Penny's Diner, Maxine's Bakery, Mrs. Dorothea's garden, past his and Mr. K's house, and down a lonely, winding road.

Yudi collapsed far away from the shiny black boots. He circled around lost, hungry, and scared of the dark. Then out of the darkness came music. Faraway and faint, but definitely Mr. K's favorite opera.

Yudi followed the sounds, limping and stumbling through the trees, until he stepped into the garden of a grand white house.

The moon shone down on Yudi through the branches of a giant walnut tree. The music stopped. The last light went out. The people in the house were all sleeping. Yudi closed his eyes, too. He dreamed he was back home on his favorite rug, getting scratched behind the ears. He dreamed he heard Mr. K saying, "You're a good one, Yudi."

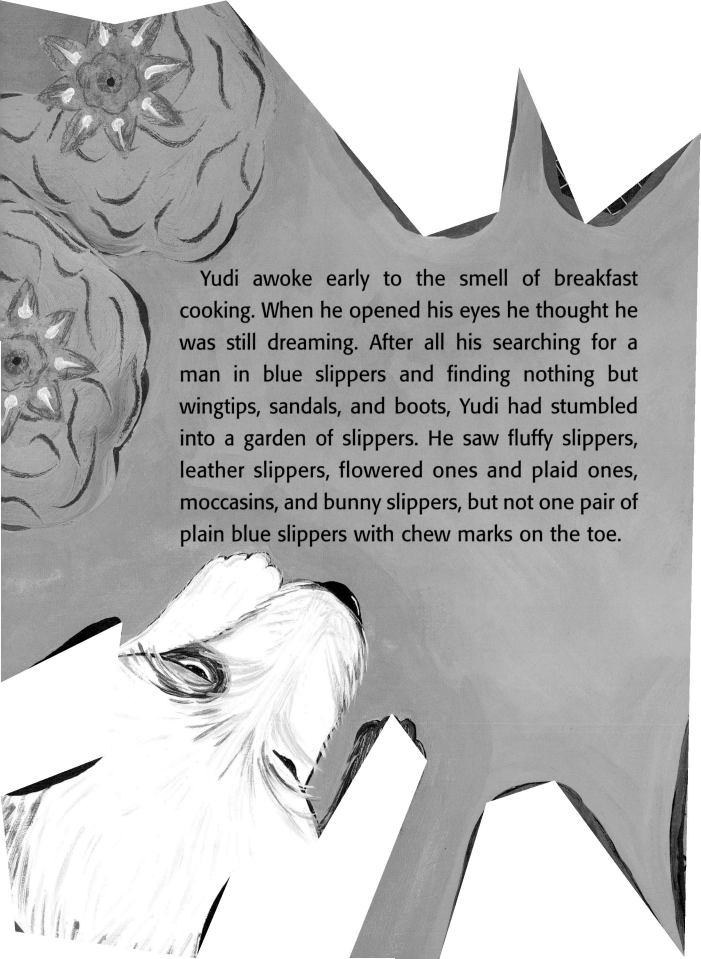

Yudi awoke early to the smell of breakfast cooking. When he opened his eyes he thought he was still dreaming. After all his searching for a man in blue slippers and finding nothing but wingtips, sandals, and boots, Yudi had stumbled into a garden of slippers. He saw fluffy slippers, leather slippers, flowered ones and plaid ones, moccasins, and bunny slippers, but not one pair of plain blue slippers with chew marks on the toe.

A man in green slippers reached down and scratched Yudi behind the ears. "Hi there, fella," the man said. "Nice to see a new face. We don't get many visitors like you, here at the rest home." He was a good man, but he was not Mr. K. Yudi hung his head and turned to leave the slipper garden.

Bump. Yudi's nose hit a rubber wheel. He looked up and saw a strange rolling chair sitting under the giant walnut tree. The man in the chair wore plain blue slippers. Yudi looked closely at the toe of the left slipper. He recognized the tiny chew marks he had put there years ago.

. K p... ...ne
ears. Th... ...ou're a
good ... ...just as he'd
...ey sat ... ...e walnut tree to
...rise.

Mr. K and Yudi were family again . . . and still the best of friends.